Alec McMillan

Divers Ditties

Chiefly written in India

Alec McMillan

Divers Ditties
Chiefly written in India

ISBN/EAN: 9783337424855

Printed in Europe, USA, Canada, Australia, Japan

Cover: Foto ©Andreas Hilbeck / pixelio.de

More available books at **www.hansebooks.com**

DIVERS DITTIES

Chiefly written in India

WITH APPENDICES

BY

ALEC M^cMILLAN M.A.

BENGAL CIVIL SERVICE

(RETIRED)

WESTMINSTER

ARCHIBALD CONSTABLE

AND CO. 1895

Edinburgh : T. and A. CONSTABLE, Printers to Her Majesty

PREFACE

NEARLY all the verses in this book appeared originally in the Allahabad *Pioneer*. I am indebted to the proprietors of that journal for permission to reproduce them in a collected form. And I have the kind permission of the proprietors of *London Society* to include the lines 'To Bonnie Bell' in my collection. I have a similar permission as regards 'Dido Anglo-Indica' from the proprietors of the *Literary World*.

As there are a good many references in the verses to experiences familiar to Magistrates and Judges in India, I have thought it not out of place to print as Appendices three papers which have a bearing on their work. These also are reproduced, with permission, from the *Pioneer*.

Readers in England, it is hoped, will take an interest in the following types, well-known to

their countrymen in India; the callow young
Civilian, disappointed at finding that the gorgeous
East is not as gorgeous as he had expected
(p. 15); the Civilian of maturer years, embittered
by long waiting for promotion (p. 90); the yet
older Civilian, encumbered by his too many
'hostages to fortune' (p. 99); the well-worn
Spinster, eager for matrimony—an end not so
easy of attainment in the India of to-day, when
marrying men can run home from Bombay in
less than three weeks, and select their partners
from the large choice the British Isles afford
(p. 77); the Grass Widow (p. 93); the fleeting
Globe-trotter (p. 122); the Hindu peasant,
patient and obsequious in the presence of autho-
rity (p. 32); the less common sort of Hindu, a
law-breaker by vocation (p. 112); the Hindu
undergoing instruction, greatly to his discomfort,
in the procedure of an English Court of Justice
(p. 43); and the lying Hindu *passim* (pp. 5, 18,
44, 45, 91, 116; App. I. and II.).

A. M.

CONTENTS

I. ORIGINAL VERSES WRITTEN IN INDIA

PAGE

Anundorum Borooah 3

Address to the Wallahs of 1869 . . 15

The Last Man in Naini Tal . . 20

The Model Alibi 25

The Hakim Bundobust . . 31

The Wohobby Horse . . 37

Trial by Assessors . 43

Disillusion 51

The Road to Pepityapore . 53

II. ORIGINAL VERSES WRITTEN IN ENGLAND

A Drinking Song . . 61

To Bonnie Bell . . 64

The Banner of Cant . . . 66

To a Lady, with a Locket . 68

The Tichborne Case . . 71

A Crux for Lispers 74

vii

CONTENTS

III. ADAPTATIONS WRITTEN IN INDIA

		PAGE
Song of the Ancient Spin	. . .	77
John Anderson and Co.	.	86
'Joint' at Two Score .	.	90
The Widow of Grass	.	93
The Civilian Obadiahs . .		96
Ye Banks and Braes o' Dehra Doon	.	103
Lament of the Settlement Officers	.	106
Alun Aheer . .	.	112
Dido Anglo-Indica	.	122
C.S.I. and C.I.E.		124
Bruce's Address : New Version	.	126

APPENDICES

i. The *Alibi* of the East	.	128
ii. Justice *à la* Bridoye for India	.	131
iii. Appeal of the Elders in the Strange Case of Susanna : An Ancient Law Report	.	136

ERRATA

p. 119, bottom line, for " in " read " an "

p. 121, top line, for " heart " read " art "

Λ

ANUNDORUM BOROOAH[1]

A RHAPSODY IN RHYME

Phœbus ! What a name
To fill the speaking trump of future fame. BYRON

THERE is a sound that haunts my ear,

That holds me with a spell of power

From sunset to the day-dawn clear,

From dawn until the sunset hour :

'Tis not the blast's autumnal roar,

'Tis not the sound of waters falling,

'Tis no sweet music loved of yore,

Lost echoes of the past recalling :

---

[1] This was the name of one of the Indian Civil Servants
selected at the open competition of 1871.

3

ANUNDORUM BOROOAH

'Tis not the strain that thrills the air
At midnight when the bulbul sings;
'Tis not the name of damsel fair:
'Tis not—a thousand other things.
In short, 'tis what you ne'er can guess.
Know, then, it's nothing more or less
Than what seven syllables express,
The name of that late-passed C.S.,
      Anundorum Borooah!

When Haileybury's hall of fame
Fell, scoffed at as an old-world sham,
And India's service first became
The meed of merit—and of cram—
We looked in course of time to see
Muir, Lawrence, ranked with Chatterjee.
And Colvins alternate with Dutts,
And Ghoses elbow Elliotts.

ANUNDORUM BOROOAH

But vengeful Heaven strike me dumb,
If e'er we thought of name so 'rum'
Tam mirum, tam magnificum
As this of thine, Anundorum,
      Anundorum Borooah!

At morn, when I to court repair,
Where day by day on judgment chair,
By dint of many a wild surmise,
I strive to strike a balance fair
Between contending sets of lies,
That eerie name pursues me there,
Mocked by all sounds that round me rise,
Droned in the Amlah's [1] monotone,
Blent with each tax appellant's moan,
And buzzing with the buzzing flies!

---

[1] 'Amlah'—native clerks who write, and read out, vernacular papers.

5

My very goose-quill, seized with craze,
Half automatically traces
Anundorum all kinds of ways,
Borooah in all sorts of places:
Like Dickens's immortal Toots,
A forger innocent of blame,
I try how large, how small-hand suits
The letters of that wondrous name,
How flourished capitals become
The signature Anundorum,
    Anundorum Borooah !

By night, when, swinging o'er my bed,
The punkah fans my weary head,
Still to the tune Anundorum
The waving fringes go and come :
And when the coolie drops the rope,
And I about my chamber grope,

ANUNDORUM BOROOAH

Irate but mute,
For brush or boot,
Or fragments of carbolic soap,
Or volumes of fat Law Digest,
As missiles to disturb his rest,
Then seem, as if by fiends possest
Mosquitoes with infernal hum
To iterate Anundorum—
Anundorum Borooah !

I sleep—that name becomes the theme
Of many a changed and troublous
dream :
Full oft, in fitful slumber tost,
I see a battle won and lost.
I hear Borooah's dread cognomen
Sound fear and death to flying foemen ;
Anon returns the conquering host,

ANUNDORUM BOROOAH

While thunders every thundering drum
Anundorum !   Anundorum !
As home they march in victor state,
A band of maidens young and gay
Comes tripping from the city gate,
And some with roses strew the way,
Some wave green palms in air, and some   .
On lutes of sounding amber thrum
The praises of Anundorum,

      Anundorum Borooah !

'Tis past,—my dream is changed,—and now
There seems beside my couch to stand,
With earnest eyes and thoughtful brow,
A Wallah, son of Scotia's land,
No Philistine, a child of light.
While such as he win India's praise,
Still Scotland, as in ancient days,

May glory in her Wallahs wight![1]
Who is it but that smart young man,
In lore of languages excelling,
Of late with a new-fangled plan
Let loose to teach all India spelling?
Him do I greet with glamorous glee,
'O mighty Hunter, LL.D!'[2]
Let Oude be spelt as heretofore,
And Kanhpur still be writ Cawnpore,
For I have work more fit for thee:
The hour is come, and thou the man
Who canst, although none other can,

[1] 'Wallahs wight.' Wight was an epithet applied to Scotland's national hero in old ballads and rhyming chronicles—

'O for one hour of Wallace wight.' SCOTT.

[2] 'Hunter, LL.D.' Now Sir W. W. Hunter, K.C.S.I. He was one of the earliest Competition Wallahs. His merits as a statistician and historian are well known. The Government of India put him in charge of the introduction of a scientific and uniform system of spelling the names of places in India.

ANUNDORUM BOROOAH

Resolve this tough conund[e]rum,
How shall we spell Anundorum,
        Anundorum Borooah ?'

In shades of visionary mist,
With look that's somewhat posed and glum,
Down sinks the etymologist,
Muttering Anundorum.
But, hist !—What second shape doth rise ?
What prescient tremor fills my breast ?
O joy ! beyond expression blest,
Borooah's self I recognise !
He smiles upon me, calls me ' Pal,'
That peerless name 's original
In mould corporeal confest ;
He deigns with me to talk and jest,
To chaff, drink pegs, and all the rest,
As man does with his brother men ;

Laughs when I ask, turned Catechist,
Who gave in lieu of M or N
That name, most strange, nost barbarous
E'er blazoned in a Civil List.
Grown bolder, I address him thus:
' You know, my Nundy, tattlers say
That, e'er you passed the other day,
You played a horoscopic hoax [1]
On our good easy English folks,
By dropping out an awkward year
In counting up your age's sum
[The evil-speaking *Pioneer*
Thus libelleth Anundorum].'
The Nundy lists with pricked-up ear,
And eyes me with an artful leer;

---

[1] ' Horoscopic hoax.' A Hindu uses his horoscope as evidence of his age. The information contained in horoscopes is not always very exact, and, so far as exact, not always accurate.

Then, parting one hand's finger-tips,
He puts unto his nose the thumb,
And drops, from scarcely opening lips,
One syllable of meaning—mum !
This said—he vanishes, and I
Awake and desolately cry,
'Where hast thou fled, my friend, my chum?—
Anundorum !   Anundorum !
Anundorum Borooah !'

Thus night by night, thus day by day,
That jarring name assails my peace,
No charm will drive the pest away,
In vain I struggle for release ;
The victim of a new disease,
To wit, Borooah on the brain,
I feel that—not by slow degrees
I grow beyond all hope insane :

ANUNDORUM BOROOAH

Soon, soon will dawn my day of doom,
When intellect's remaining spark
Shall fail, and leave me in the dark
To sink into an early tomb.
The friends I leave behind to weep
Will raise a tablet—chaste tho' cheap—
To mark their grief—at moderate cost—
For one so young, so early lost;
And, graven on the marble cold,
My piteous tale shall thus be told :—
' Here rests, by trouble vexed no more,
The bard of Sabsechotapore ;
He lived beloved, he died demented,—
Killed by a name of sound more wild
Than e'er was for a fork-tailed child
In Pandæmonium invented !
Time was he trolled a merry note ;
Now death has stilled his tuneful throat,

Has bid his lyric lips be dumb ;
Woe worth the day that weird sound smote
On his astounded tympanum !
Then, traveller, pause, let fall a tear,
And backwards read recorded here
The name of doom, the name of fear,
Anundorum, Anundorum !
The king of sounds, uncouth and queer,
Of all that can revolt the ear,
Cacophonous compendium,
      Anundorum Borooah,
Anundorum, Anundorum,
      Anundorum Borooah ! '

ADDRESS TO THE WALLAHS OF 1869

BY A [COMPARATIVELY] OLD WALLAH

[Fifty Competition Wallahs were selected in 1869.
Four of them, one named Gupta and three others,
were natives of India.]

Of schools, of cramming dens the choice,
   O Wallahs new, a goodly band,
Fain would I lift a warning voice
   To turn you from this promised land.
I speak not to the Hindus four,
   The gifted Gupta and the rest;
Let them breathe Indian air once more,
   It's bad enough to suit them best.

15

But you, ye forty-six, give ear,
    Who now in days of ease enjoy
The praise of friends and parents dear,
    Exulting in their darling boy :
List, list to me, while still there's time,
    Ere yet you tempt the Indian shore,
Nor spurn, though couched in homely
        rhyme,
His warning who has gone before.

Go starve as usher in a school,
    Go study briefless at the bar,
Or mount a merchant's office stool,
    Or don the scarlet garb of war :
Go cultivate the Grub Street Muse,
    Go preach for forty younds a year,
Go sweep a crossing, cobble shoes,
    But don't, my brethren, don't come here !

16

'Twas but three fleeting years ago
  I passed the ordeal dread like you,
And panted, all my heart aglow,
  To rule with love the mild Hindoo ;
My step was light, my arm was strong,
  The pride of hope lit up my brow ;
I dreamt of glory all day long :
  Such was I then—behold me now !

Here in a dried-up desert spot,
  To white heat burnt by India's sun,
Six lonely wights bemoan their lot,
  All banished men, and I am one.
No more for me the zest, the charm,
  That hopes of praise and fame inspire ;
In fact I find it far too warm
  To set old Gunga Jee [1] on fire.

[1] ' Gunga Jee '—the river Ganges.

All day I swelter in my chair,
  Administ'ring the law's redress,
Bewildered, dazed, provoked to swear
  By perjured 'clouds of witnesses.'
Lord! how they lie, unmoved by fear
  Of all their million ugly gods;
I make out scarcely half I hear,
  But then it's lies, so what's the odds?

What remnant Fund deductions spare,
  Unmulcted, of my monthly pay,
My bearer and Khansamah share;
  It's got and gone the self-same day.
My liver hour by hour expands,
  The syces eat my horse's gram,[1]
The merc'ry o'er a hundred stands,
  And I've to read for next exam.

[1] 'Gram'—a sort of pea on which horses are fed in India in place of oats.

18

My ruddy cheeks have long grown pale
   Beneath the sun's relentless fire,
I dare not drink a glass of ale,
   And those damned seniors won't retire.
Black scorpions infest my shoes,
   Ants batten on my best-loved books,
And last home mail brought out the news
   My Maud had wed that blockhead Snooks.

Then I have fever at odd times,
   By way of change from prickly heat ;
I could not in a thousand rhymes
   The list of India's ills complete.
Mosquitoes fell are left unsung,
   Official flouts, and snubs, and kicks ;
O listen to my warning tongue,
   And stay at home, ye forty-six !

THE LAST MAN IN NAINI TAL

Naini Tal is a favourite hill station in the North-West
Provinces. Its fashionable season closes early in
November.

'Tis chilly eve as forth I stray,
    A lonely pilgrim sad and slow,
And one by one the scenes survey,
    So changed since six short weeks ago.

The club is hushed; no roisterers come
    And throng its festal board at eight,
And throw the rude but harmless crumb,
    Or hurl the not quite harmless plate.[1]

[1] 'The not quite harmless plate.' It is only fair to say that
an isolated incident is referred to here. Plate-propelling is
not a *customary* dinner-table pastime in the Naini Tal Club.

20

THE LAST MAN IN NAINI TAL

The servants with the sahibs are fled :
    A last lone kit,—there's left but one,—
With shameless and unturbaned head
    Sits out to catch the evening sun.

Now on the Mall no dandies throng,
    Nor shapely damsels spur apace ;
Save when some coolie plods along
    You cannot see a human face.

No orderly in red and gold
    Sets down his box of 'urgent files,'
And, heedless though the day grows old,
    With loitering ayah chats and smiles.

The lake is cold and bleak and bare ;
    No toiling crews of rival fours,
Steered by the hands of coxswains fair,
    Upturn the wave with gleaming oars.

No paired canoers, side by side
   Close drifting in the gloaming dim,
Make passing oarsmen, Argus-eyed,
   Take curious note of *her* and *him*.

The library no sound doth stir ;
   No lovers in its furtive nooks
Their own low whispered talk prefer
   To all that's writ in prosy books.

Hushed is the stage where many a night
   Our actors, Thespian vot'ries true,
Their own dear selves did much delight,
   And [sometimes] pleased their audience too.

No more to Morrison's repair
   Stray buyers, tempted as they pass,
No longer on his weighing-chair
   Sits portly dame or lissome lass ;

THE LAST MAN IN NAINI TAL

The spins, 'unprofitably gay,'
    Who glittered all the season through,
Spins[1] as they came have gone their
       way ;
    In Naini Tal they mostly do !

Whether they have themselves to blame,
    Some over fast, some too sedate,
Or frisky matrons spoil their game,
    Let graver pens than mine debate ;

Howe'er that be, October sere
    Has closed the season's good and ill ;
The last fond lapdog cavalier
    Has seen his lady down the hill.

---

[1] 'Spins.' Unmarried and [more or less] marriageable ladies are called spins in India—short for spinsters.

THE LAST MAN IN NAINI TAL

No more as in the six months past
   These hills a moving drama show ;
I 've marked its phases to the last,
   The curtain's fall'n, it 's time to go.

Hi, bearer !   I 'll no longer stay ;
   Haste to the thana,[1] coolies call ;
The setting of to-morrow's day
   Must see me far from Naini Tal.

[1] 'Thana '—police station.

THE MODEL ALIBI.

By Jones of the Thinner Temple. [*See Appendix* I.]

'Twas brought to me by Kumbukht Khan,
    A rising young Mukhtar,
And Rummun Lal, the smartest man
    In all the Hindu bar.

They said : ' This Alibi behold,
    A model of its kind ' ;
Its flawless beauty they extolled,
    With care and art designed,

And vowed its finish was so fine,
    Wrought out in such a sort,
No hand less skilled, less light than mine,
    Could take it up in Court.

'But is it genuine,' said I,
    'No put up thing, you know?'
With ready smile they made reply:
    'We are instructed so.'

'That's right—instructions always plead;
    They fence our honour in—
A very useful fence indeed,
    Though sometimes rather thin.'

The case was one of murder red,
    A Banya stabbed and slain;
For this the kin who mourned him dead
    Did Bundur Singh arraign.

Now Bundur ne'er in all his life—
    So my instructions ran—
Had raised his hand, far less a knife,
    To smite a fellow-man.

26

THE MODEL ALIBI

The deed, besides, at Sonk was done,
    And Bundur on that day
To Tonk had sped ere rose the sun,
    Good twenty miles away.

At dawn a pair of country kine
    He bought in Tonk Bazaar,
At Tonk Dispensary at nine
    Got dosed for a catarrh ;

At noon with Tonk's most rev'rend priest
    He stayed for midday rest,
At sunset at a birthday feast
    Sat down, an honoured guest ;

At night with trusty cousins twain,
    He slept at Tonk Serai,
Next day by train went home again :
    A lovely Alibi !

27

THE MODEL ALIBI

I took it to the Sessions Judge,
    But, though I talked my best,
He seemed to hear with listless ear,
    Nor looked the least impressed.

The model Alibi in vain
    I lauded to the skies:
The Judge was stone—it found, 'twas plain,
    No favour in his eyes.

With rough rude hand, with rough rude wit,
    He held it up to view:
Its joinings delicately knit
    He poked his fingers through;

And as he scanned it o'er and o'er
    He said, 'It's not amiss,
But I've seen Alibis ten score,
    As good—or bad—as this.'

And then that peerless Alibi
    Right out of doors he flung,
And doomed poor Bundur Singh to die,
    By cord and noose up strung !

No matter !   Art that's exquisite
    Strikes not the purblind eye ;
As lower Courts are dull of sight
    I'll seek the Court that's High.

The Weekly Notes will scraps provide
    My model to repair,
And Full Bench rulings well applied
    Will patch each rent and tear.

The good old Court, I know, will say
    The Sessions Judge was wrong
To treat in such a scoffing way
    An Alibi so strong.

With mazy windings, in and out,
    They'll argue con and pro,
Then rule there's room at least for doubt,
    And let my Bundur go.

And Bundur free a good round fee
    Will surely not deny:
And blithe we'll join in blessing thee
    My own, my Alibi!

> 'Men may come and men may go,
>   But I go on for ever.'

> 'He was not for an age, but for all time.'

Hakim Bundobust means Settlement Officer, that is to say, an officer who assesses the revenue to be paid to Government by owners of land.   These verses were originally published in the *Pioneer* with the following preamble :—

'There is a district in these provinces in which a meritorious officer, under colour of making a periodical settlement of the land revenue, has, to all appearances, permanently settled himself. His operations have already been prolonged beyond the ordinary term, yet there is no sign of their drawing to a close. The native inhabitants of the district have become gradually impressed with the idea that no living man

31

will see the completion of the settlement. When they wish to express that a particular debt will never be recovered, they say it will be paid " when the settlement is finished." The common feeling of the people on the subject has found expression in a kind of rude prophetic poem, the work of some village genius. Of the original Hindee of that poem the following stanzas are a tolerably literal translation. It is commonly sung at funeral ceremonies by the kinsmen of the deceased, and nothing can be more inexpressibly touching than the weary and monotonous wail with which the band of mourners take up the refrain. Once heard it is not likely to be forgotten.'

I

YOUNG BUGGOO, king of scarecrow boys,
Stands sentry o'er his father's grain,
And screams all day with might and main,
        Exulting in the noise:
But see! why doth he turn about,
Forget his charge, and cease to shout?

32

THE HAKIM BUNDOBUST

It is because the Sahib comes,
The serious Sahib, staid and slow,
Who plods the village to and fro,
And jots down notes and tots up sums—
  The Hakim Bundobust.

II

Ten years see Buggoo grown a man :
Of all the reapers, ten abreast,
He wields the busy sickle best,
  And deftly leads the van.
But see ! why doth he stay his hand,
And rev'rently attentive stand ?
It is because the Sahib comes,
The serious Sahib, staid and slow,
Who plods the village to and fro,
And jots down notes and tots up sums—
  The Hakim Bundobust.

III

Old age has grizzled Buggoo's head ;
His years of lusty labour done,
Now sits he dreaming in the sun
    Of youth for ever fled :
But see ! he opes his half-shut eyes,
And strains his aching limbs to rise.
It is because the Sahib comes,
The serious Sahib, staid and slow,
Who plods the village to and fro,
And jots down notes and tots up sums—
    The Hakim Bundobust.

IV

Old Buggoo 's dead.   His sons their sire
Swift to the holy river take,
And singe him for their conscience' sake
    With scantly fuelled fire.

THE HAKIM BUNDOBUST

Then launch him in the waters—there
To float in peace, nor longer care
Though still the self-same Sahib comes,
The serious Sahib, staid and slow,
Who plods the village to and fro,
And jots down notes and tots up sums—
      The Hakim Bundobust.

v

The changing seasons come and go :
The Buggoos whom we looked upon
But yesterday, to-day are gone ;
      But this we surely know,
Till our eyes too in death grow dim
We ne'er shall see the last of him
Who still, interminably slow,
Plods, plods the village to and fro,

35

THE HAKIM BUNDOBUST

And jots down notes and tots up sums,
Who never, like the drought and rust,
Desisteth, but unfailing comes—
>The Hakim Bundobust.

THE WOHOBBY HORSE

[In 1871 Dr. Hunter—see one of the notes to 'Anundorum Borooah'—published a book in which Mohammedans of the Wahabi sect were represented as very terrible and dangerous persons. An effective reply to Dr. Hunter's views was written by Syed Ahmad Khan, now Sir Syed Ahmad, a respected member of the Mohammedan community.]

O ONCE there lived a hunter,

Who wrought a cruel joke ;

He built a big Wohobby horse

To scare douce, honest folk.

Its shape in carven timber

All hollow he expressed,

As one who knew the adage true—

' Things hollow sound the best.'

37

THE WOHOBBY HORSE

And next, like Greek Apelles,
   He painted it so well,
It looked a steed of demon breed
   Just fresh arrived from h—ll.

Its flanks of raven darkness
   Were dashed with gouts of blood ;
Like steel of proof, each shining hoof,
   Belied the hollow wood.

Thick smoke from out its nostrils wide
   Or seemed to come or came ;
It glared with anger, fiery-eyed ;
   Its mane and tail were flame.

And when the beast was ready
   The hunter it bestrode,
And, flushed with pride, did wildly ride
   All down the Mecca road.

THE WOHOBBY HORSE

Was never steed so wilful!
  No rein would hold it in:
O'errock it dashed, through mire it plashed,
  With dire portentous din,

And, marvel of all marvels
  That ever yet was known,
No other force impelled its course
  But empty wind alone!

And folk in crowds came running
  The loud turmoil to hear,
And eyed agape the grisly shape
  And shook with boding fear.

But so it chanced thereafter
  That rain began to pour,
And drenched, alack! the charger's back
  And marred the dyes it wore.

Its wooden knees protruded bare
No longer glorious-hued ;
Its ribs of deal were seen to stare
Unlovely, 'in the nude.'

In short, of all its lies undressed,
Its tints all disarrayed,
It stood to ev'ry eye confessed
A wretched wooden jade.

This sudden change beholding
That came the monster o'er,
The gazing crowd laughed long and loud,
Nor quaked in terror more.

And up there rose a Syed,
A sage with hoary head
(They called him Khan, a canny man),
And this was what he said—

THE WOHOBBY HORSE

'Get down, get down, Sir Hunter,
    From that Wohobby beast:
You ride apace a wild-goose chase,
    Nor know your road the least.

' 'Tis sham, your art fantastic,
    That specious outward seems;—
Your horse, I wis, a nightmare is,
    Its rider's daft, and dreams.

' Be wise, and to your own Bengal
    Return, nor hold it true,
That who has drawn a black Southal
    Can paint Wohobbies too.'

Thus did the Syed counsel;
    But, after, what befell,
Or what, thus chid, the hunter did,
    My story fails to tell.

But all whom dyed Wohobbies please,
  Mark you the moral plain,
And ride beneath your own roof-trees—
  Not outside in the rain.

TRIAL BY ASSESSORS

FRAGMENT OF AN UNPUBLISHED DRAMA

'The Court shall require each of the Assessors to state his opinion orally, and shall record such opinion. The Judge shall not be bound to conform to the opinions of the Assessors.'—*Code of Criminal Procedure.*

'While avoiding prolixity, a Sessions Judge should be careful to be intelligible and precise in recording the opinions of Assessors.'—*High Court Circular.*

THE JUDGE

Sir Assessor Gunga Singh,
Yawning, dozing, fidgeting,
With a bored and weary air,
Sir Assessor Mukhun Ram,
Writhing with uneasy ham
On an unaccustomed chair,

43

The end of these proceedings slow
Is near, as you 'll rejoice to know :
And, all else done, 'tis now your place
To state your views upon the case :
They matter not one little d—n,
Gunga Singh and Mukhun Ram,
But seeing that the law expects
This effort from your intellects,
State your verdict, have your fling,
Mukhun Ram and Gunga Singh.

The charge is murder, rank, blood-red :
Five Chumars on oath have said
That Poorun Thakur, the accused,
Because Duleep Chumar refused
To weed his cane-field, smote him dead
With murd'rous axe-blow on the head.

44

TRIAL BY ASSESSORS

This tragedy took place, they swore,
At dawn of day in Toodulpore.
The time they told this tale of blood
You, Mukhun Ram, in absent mood
Were scratching with a fatuous grin
The ancient boilmarks on your shin.

Next came the case for the defence :
Thakurs ten gave evidence
That on the day this blood was shed
Poorun in the morning grey
Miles from Toodulpore away,
Miles beyond the Jumna far,
Was buying at the Dhond Bazaar
A milk-white cow with one ear red.

While thus the Thakurs ten deposed
You, Gunga Singh, serenely dozed,

Till, starting up with smothered snore,
You nearly tumbled on the floor.
The testimony, pro and con,
Exercise your minds upon,
And to this question answer, say,
Is Poorun guilty? Yea or nay?
Shall he be absolved or swing,
Mukhun Ram and Gunga Singh?

ASSESSOR MUKHUN RAM

What can this humble slave reply
Except *jo kooch huzoor ka rai.*[1]

ASSESSOR GUNGA SINGH

And what decide this bondsman poor
But only just *jo rai huzoor.*[1]

---

[1] 'Jo kooch huzoor ka rai.' 'Jo rai huzoor.'—Whatever is
the opinion of your Highness.

TRIAL BY ASSESSORS

Very much surprised I am,
Gunga Singh and Mukhun Ram;
This is a most shocking thing,
Mukhun Ram and Gunga Singh:
What think you will the High Court
    say,
If in this abject, doltish way
You make your function high a sham,
Gunga Singh and Mukhun Ram?
Make another effort, pray,
And haste, for time is on the wing,
And when the Court adjourns to-day
It has a tennis match to play,
Mukhun Ram and Gunga Singh.

  [*The Assessors consult together.*]

.   .

47

BOTH ASSESSORS

These suppliants now would crave to tell
Their verdict to the Presence.

THE JUDGE

Well?

ASSESSOR MUKHUN RAM

The milk-white cow if Poorun bought
'Twas some one else the murder wrought.

ASSESSOR GUNGA SINGH

But if 'twas he, we think as how
It's plain he didn't buy the cow.

BOTH ASSESSORS

And one thing most of all is clear . . .

TRIAL BY ASSESSORS

THE JUDGE

I 'm all attention, let me hear.

BOTH ASSESSORS

The milk-white cow had one red car !

THE JUDGE

Assessors, with due meed of praise
Your verdict sage I must commend :
Like two-edged sword, it cuts both ways
And has a keen and pointed end.
Engrossed on creamy foolscap fair
I 'll send it to the High Court—there
The upright Judge whom men call Straight[1]
Will give it due regard and weight

---

[1] 'Whom men call Straight.'—Mr. Justice Straight, for some years a Puisne Judge in the Allahabad High Court ; now Sir Douglas Straight.

Or e'er in Poorun's case he saith

The final word, release or death.

And now, my friends, you may depart,

I thank you both with all my heart,

And trust that fortune still may bring,

As oft as on the bench I sit

Assessors as approved and fit,

Assessors of as searching wit

As Mukhun Ram and Gunga Singh.

Note.—In Sessions Districts in India into which trial by jury has not been introduced the Legislature inflicts on Judges the burden of the presence of Assessors. The Assessors would much rather be at their own homes than in the Judge's cutcherry. Their opinions and reasons are often so foolish that it is the merest waste of time to record them. In what are looked upon as advanced districts, jurymen sit with the Judge instead of Assessors. Jurymen are sometimes as foolish as Assessors, and they can do much more harm ; for whereas the Judge need not conform to the opinion of Assessors, he is bound by law to give judgment in accordance with the verdict—however foolish or perverse—of a jury.

DISILLUSION

These verses appeared in *The Pioneer* with the following heading :—

'The indefatigable Head of the Police in these Provinces has issued a circular of twenty-three pages on the subject of the dress and equipment of "The Force." The following passages are extracted from two pages of minute description of the Full Dress Uniform Coat :—"'Two pleats under the breast pockets to give shape to the waist and fulness to the breast. . . . Coat to be lined with khaki Italian cloth, quilted on the chest and under the arms. . . . Price, Rs. 25 ; procurable from Haji Nur Bakhsh, Hazratganj, Lucknow."'

WITH look of pride upon his face

He stood, like martial hero drest ;

Well pleased I marked each manly grace,

And most of all his ample chest.

51

DISILLUSION

I saw and loved ; but, woe is me !
   The charms that caught my dazzled eyes
Were those that for a modest fee
   A shop in Hazratganj supplies.

A sham my padded hero's heart
   By quilted pleating overlaid,
Not nature gave him shape, but art,—
   His swelling chest was tailor-made.

Ye maids, who pine for love and truth,
   A sister's warning voice believe ;
Beware the gallant peeler youth,
   He charms, but oh ! his charms deceive.

THE ROAD TO PEPITYAPORE

AN IDYLL OF CAMP LIFE IN INDIA

'Frequent and unreserved intercourse with all classes of
the community is most necessary for the efficient performance
of a Collector's duties. Nothing tends more to promote this
than the habit of constantly moving about the district during
the cold season.'—*Directions for Collectors*, para. 25.

IT was long years ago, when cutcherry was
    done,
As I wandered from camp with my dog and my
    gun,
        The fields for a shot to explore,
A comeliest damsel I chanced to espy
All under the shade of a tamarind high
        On the road to Pepityapore.

53

THE ROAD TO PEPITYAPORE

In the stately repose of a ripe womanhood,
With the grace of a goddess of Hellas she stood,
    And the glory of summers a score,
Fronting the sun that to setting was nigh,
All under the shade of a tamarind high,
    On the road to Pepityapore.

So proud was her presence, so winsome her
    air,
That drawn by the glamour of vision so fair,
    My purpose of sport I forebore ;
And to see her the nearer and hear her reply,
I asked her the road from that tamarind high
    To the town of Pepityapore.

A saree of blue with a border of red
Made a robe for her figure, a hood for her head,
    The only apparel she wore ;

THE ROAD TO PEPITYAPORE

And frankly she answered, not shrinking and shy,
When I asked her the road from that tamarind
high
To the town of Pepityapore.

Rude trinkets and poor on the dark of her arm,—
Its hue as of bronze, but a bronze glowing
warm,—
Shone bright as the costliest ore;
And never flashed gem like her dark beaming
eye,
All under the shade of the tamarind high,
On the road to Pepityapore.

Her speech was a patois, mine learnt out of books,
So we talked less by words than the language of
looks,
And it took us an hour, ay and more,

THE ROAD TO PEPITYAPORE

While swiftly, too swiftly, the time seemed to fly,
As she taught me, all under the tamarind high,
   The road to Pepityapore.

But sudden at last, with a gesture of fear,
She whispered, 'See yonder, my husband is near.
   Depart ere he comes, I implore.'
Thus bidden, I breathed but a hasty good-bye,
And left her alone by the tamarind high,
   On the road to Pepityapore.

The husband approached; he was dhotied[1] and
   grey,
I watched from afar as he led her away,
   And plainly perceived that he swore,

[1] 'Dhotied.'—This is not a misprint for 'doted.' A dhoti is a garment worn by all Hindus, and it is the favourite, and often the only, wear of the poorer classes.

56

THE ROAD TO PEPITYAPORE

In a fret and a fume at the wherefore and why
Of her lagging so late by the tamarind high
    On the road to Pepityapore.

Next evening again, when cutcherry was done,
I followed, nor called for my dog or my gun,
    The path of the evening before;
But vainly I watched till the stars lit the sky,
She came not again to the tamarind high,
    On the road to Pepityapore.

It was long years ago; what her lot may now be
I know not, nor ever shall know—as for me,
    I'm tied to a wife—she's a bore;
And I've never told her, and I don't mean to
      try,
Of the damsel I met by the tamarind high,
    On the road to Pepityapore.

THE ROAD TO PEPITYAPORE

But often in camp when the day's work is sped,
As I sit by my fire with the stars overhead,
    Old memories pondering o'er,
I think of the lass with the dark beaming eye,
And swear to hold dear till I drivel or die
That sweetest of hours by the tamarind high,
    On the road to Pepityapore.

['The Road to Pepityapore' has been set to music by
Captain T. H. Bairnsfather, IX Punjáb Infantry, and published by Messrs. Alfred Hays and Co., Old Bond Street.]

II

ORIGINAL VERSES WRITTEN
IN ENGLAND

A DRINKING SONG

Come, lads, join in with chorus strong,
  Let care be flung aside,
While we in joys of wine and song
  All mortal dole deride.

Behold the toiling human race,
  By fevered hopes possest ;
Delusions vain intent to chase,
  They know nor peace nor rest.

The lover for a maiden burns,
  And sighs his life away,
Or rues when humdrum Hymen turns
  His goddess into clay.

A DRINKING SONG

The poet pines for laurelled fame,
   His cankered brow to bind ;
His quest is but an empty name,
   That fleeteth as the wind.

The sage weighs down his weary brain
   With load of leaden lore,
That later men may reap the gain
   Of all he toils to store.

' Gold ! Gold ! More gold !' the miser cries,
   Of nobler aims devoid,
And, dying, looks with anguished eyes
   On riches unenjoyed.

The shallow preacher wastes his breath ;
   Fond guide of fools as fond,
He fain would raise the veil of death,
   And bare its dark beyond.

A DRINKING SONG

When all the best is preached and said,
  Or truth or guesses bold,
What worth has love to charm the dead,
  Or lore, or fame, or gold ?

On us no dogmas grim intrude,
  No priests our peace annoy ;
Short is our creed—that Joy is Good,
  And Wine's the Spring of Joy !

In life we chase no bubbles vain,
  In death we find no fear,
Whate'er its unknown deeps contain,
  At least we're happy here.

So lads, join in with chorus strong,
  Let care be flung aside,
While we in joys of wine and song
  All mortal dole deride !

63

WHEN first I knew thee, Bonnie Bell,
   Thy cheek with Nature's roses glowed,
The golden locks I loved so well
   In unadorned luxuriance flowed ;
Thy gentle eyes of heaven's own hue
   Threw glances innocent of art,
And mirrored in their depths of blue
   Each movement of thy guileless heart.

But all is changed now, Bonnie Bell—
   That piled up hair, those clust'ring curls,
With store of borrowed tresses swell
   That once were some poor peasant girl's ;

64

TO BONNIE BELL

The stain of carmine ill supplies
  The banished grace of blushes red ;
And where truth only lit thine eyes
  False belladonna gleams instead.

When first I loved thee, Bonnie Bell,
  And for my love no favour found,
My heart sustained the anguish fell
  Of what I deemed a deadly wound ;
But since I 've seen thine every charm
  Debased into a painted lie,
I feel my heart is healed from harm,
  And bid my pain and thee good-bye.

THE BANNER OF CANT

THE many are wicked, and we are the saints,
Whose merits a sweet self-complacency paints ;
Mankind to make moral we burn and we pant
Who follow devoted the banner of Cant.

We care not for logic ; we make no pretence
To temper our zeal with discretion or sense ;
If you challenge our aims we don't reason, we rant,
Who follow devoted the banner of Cant.

We care much for virtue ; the sum of our care
Is to hunt vice from one place and drive it else-
        where ;
We care not to kill it, we only transplant,
Who follow devoted the banner of Cant.

THE BANNER OF CANT

We care not for Freedom, our Puritan rule
Treats grown men and women like children at
  school,
And we break in on mirth with our shriek
  resonant,
Who follow devoted the banner of Cant.

We care not for toilers who slave for their bread,
Their pleadings for pity, the tears they may shed ;
Our virtue's abundant, our charity scant,
While we follow devoted the banner of Cant.

Our evangel is this, that each Pharisee fad
Shall have sway as a touchstone of good and of
  bad ;
Of this gospel let each be a hierophant
Who follows devoted the banner of Cant.

TO A LADY

I SEND thee, love, a keepsake curl,
Encased in gold, with stones of pearl
And turquoise set,—not in the thought
The gift itself containeth aught
That's worthy her to whom 'tis sent,
But rather in the fond intent
That pearl and turquoise, gold and hair,
May each a hidden meaning bear;
The yellow ore's the sign I hold
Thy love more dear than priceless gold;
The stainless pearls in symbol say
My flame for thee is pure as they:

68

TO A LADY

The emblem stones of lucent blue
Recall by their ethereal hue
The dome serene of heaven above,
That frowns on lovers false to love :
And as this rock of raven shade
Will never change its hue or fade,
Though age may blanche all snowy white
The head it left but yesternight,
E'en thus by time, by absence tried,
Unchanging shall my faith abide.
Know, then, my gift in every part,
By fancy and affection's art,
Designed to make thee think at times
Upon the singer of these rhymes.
Oh ! wear it still thine own heart near,
From day to day, from year to year,
And shouldst thou ever—O the bliss !—
Imprint upon the gold a kiss,

TO A LADY

Then shall my heart with gladness dance,
For surely by love's clairvoyance
(Though rivers wide, though mountains high,
And miles of earth between us lie)
Fleet wafted shall the message be,
My love, my love, remembers me!
And I shall prove as truly mine
The joy most near to joys divine
Of all by God vouchsafed to men—
To love and to be loved again!

THE TICHBORNE CASE

[These stanzas were written when Ballantine and Coleridge (afterwards Lord Coleridge) were engaged against one another in the Tichborne-Orton case.]

TH1s Ballantine and Orton tale
That gives the dailies ready sale,
The ceaseless topic (slightly stale)
 We day by day discourse on,
Recalls a story—lang, lang syne,
A well-thumbed favourite of mine—
About a gentle Valentine
 Who had a brother Orson.

71

The older tale my childhood knew
In bold, effective colours drew
Two pictures of contrasted hue,
 A graceful and a coarse one :
So the lost heir of Tichborne lands,
Depicted by two master hands,
Before our eyes alternate stands—
 Now Valentine, now Orson.

Hear Ballantine : Young Roger's shown
A boy with low associates thrown,
A loutish lad, a lout upgrown,
As drunk, by whiles, as Porson.
Hear Coleridge : He's a pleasing youth,
Who studied books and spoke the
  truth—
A kind of Valentine, in sooth,
 Or more like him than Orson.

THE TICHBORNE CASE

This limner draws with matchless art
A contrast, that a counterpart
To one whom, butcher born or Bart.,
    Good men should shut their doors on;
Tichborne or Orton, known for sure
In ways an Orson and a boor,
Without the heart from baseness pure
    That gave a grace to Orson.

A CRUX FOR LISPERS

SETH loves Susie, Susie Seth,
  Yet each the other freezeth :
''Tis Seth is shy,' doth Susie sigh,
  ''Tis Susie's icy,' he saith.

[The above may be regarded as a pendant to 'I saw Esau
  kissing Kate,' etc., quoted in Appendix I.]

ADAPTATIONS WRITTEN IN INDIA

SONG OF THE ANCIENT SPIN

A LONG WAY AFTER 'THE SONG OF THE SHIRT'

[See note to 'The Last Man in Naini Tal' for meaning of 'Spin.']

> 'Alacke ! a many more like her
> Doe pant with craving fonde
> To weather bleake Cape Spinisterre
> And rest in Hymen's harbour faire
> That lieth calm beyonde.'
> *Quarrelette of Quippes*: JOHN SOUTHCLIFFE.

WITH a brow of unwomanly brass

And a *triste* but tearless eye,

A lady sat at her toilet glass

As the dinner-hour drew nigh :

77

SONG OF THE ANCIENT SPIN

Her looks were a little the worse for wear
   And her voice rang treble and thin,
As she sang, with a weary and desolate air,
   The Song of the Ancient Spin.

'To smirk, smirk, smirk,
   For a lover, a ring, and a roof;
To smirk, smirk, smirk,
   Is my task for each fool's behoof;
To rattle and rally and laugh
   In an airily girlish strain,
And to bandy outworn, witless chaff
   With each bachelor dolt inane.

'And to flirt, flirt, flirt,
   With each casual random "him,"
Be he handsome or plain, be he silly or sane,
   Be he Charley, or Harry, or Jim;

78

SONG OF THE ANCIENT SPIN

Whate'er be the manner of man,
  Be he soldier, civilian, or priest,
If he's only a male in society's pale,
  Naught else is of moment the least.

'Unstinted on every one
  My catholic smiles are shed,
On widowers mourning and lone,
  On bachelors waiting to wed ;
And at times with your Benedicks tame—
  'Tis in sooth but a venial sin—
I flirt without aim, save for love of the game,
  To keep my hand well in.

'Yet no goal for my striving appears,
  And my mirror, with pitiless truth,
Shows ever the more of the ravage of years,
  Shows less of the glory of youth.

79

SONG OF THE ANCIENT SPIN

Ah! 'tis well when one's bloom is so
    hard to keep,
  And one's hair wears sparse and
    sear,
That natural tresses are held so cheap,
  And that fringes don't sell dear.

'My labour never doth slack,
  And what are its gains, all told:
That I'm chilled by the sneer of your
    dames severe,
  Who brand me as brazen and bold;
That I'm mocked at by men in a thou-
    sand of ways,
  And know that behind my back
They call me the Light of other
    Days,
  They dub me the Station Hack.

' And to-day came in, mincing, to call,
   Mary Blossom, a seven weeks' bride,
And harped on her house and her husband
     and all,
Till I felt myself brimming with angry
     gall
   At the doll-faced matron's pride;
It was more, I swear, than a saint could
     stand,
   When the little conceited thing
Got toying one flabby and gloveless hand
   To twit me with her ring.

' Yet I smirk—smirk—smirk
   In the ball-room's garish light,
.'Neath the preacher's eye at kirk,
   On the tennis lawn sun-bright.

At kirk, or tennis, or ball,
  Ball, or tennis, or kirk,
I smirk as I play, as I dance—if I pray
  I sink on my knees with a smirk.

' Woe's me for the time bygone,
  When my 'teens were scarce sped through,
And my cheek that is now so blanched and wan
  Glowed red with an English hue ;
When I numbered my gallants a score,
  And a wooer or two in the throng,—
But I cast them all by and sat waiting for more,
  Till I waited, alas ! too long.

' Came one with a fair young face,
  Harry Dare of the Onety-Oneth,
But my dreams were of riches and place,
  And he hadn't two hundred a month ;

So I silenced his suit with a "No,"
    Half sorry, half proud of his pain,
Indulged in sweet penitent woe
    For a week—and went flirting again.

'Then he was all unknown,
    Now he has earned a name,
And the praise of his valour is proudly shown
    On the glittering rolls of fame ;—
And he's married—for time saw peace return
    To his soul, and another gained
The treasure of love I was thriftless to spurn,
    The heart that I disdained.

'I saw them one festival day,
    Him and his bride, the twain,
And I watched them by stealth till I turned
        away
    With a sickened and reeling brain :

SONG OF THE ANCIENT SPIN

For I thought of old memories lost and dead,
   And of all that might have been,
Till I hated that other who stood in my stead
   For her happy and smiling mien.

'Thus Pride is punished by Fate,
   And the Nemesis comes with time
On the maiden who rueth all too late
   The waste of her misused prime ;
When her summers tide on to the triple of ten,
   And she 's banned by the general voice
As despised and rejected of men,
   And a spinster not by choice.

'Oh for but one short hour !
   A respite, however brief,
From a life that hath neither love nor hope,
   Nor one ennobling grief !

SONG OF THE ANCIENT SPIN

A little weeping would ease my soul,
   But the tears must never be shed,
For how could I play the Siren's *rôle*
   With eyelids heavy and red?'

With a brow of unwomanly brass,
   And a *triste* but tearless eye,
The lady rose from her toilet glass,
   Sighing a deep-drawn sigh :
O'er many a wretch the blue skies bend
   In this weariful world of sin,
But few be there ever—so Heaven forfend !—
Weary as she, without hope, without friend,
Singing, and fated to sing to the end,
   The Song of the Ancient Spin.

JOHN ANDERSON AND CO.

Air—'*John Anderson, my jo.*'

In the earlier 'Seventies Anderson and Co. were a well-known Calcutta firm, dealing in tinned provisions and other necessaries of Indian housekeeping.

The penniless Poet is dunned. He appealeth to the Purveyor.

John Anderson an' Co., John,
 When we were first acquent,
On wares o' thine sae dainty
 My siller fain was spent ;
But noo my siller's gane, John,
 My credit's unco low,
Ye maunna fash me sair for cash,
 John Anderson an' Co.

86

JOHN ANDERSON AND CO.

John Anderson an' Co., John,
   A paction let us mak,
For a' the wares ye send me
   In rhyme I'll pay ye back;
As with a trumpet-blast, John,
   Thy fame abroad I'll blow,
Till far an' near the warl' shall hear
   Of Anderson an' Co.

Thy hams in cunning tins, John,
   How passing sweet and prime!
Thy name will keep as sweet for aye,
   Enshrined in living rhyme;
And down to days unborn, John,
   In glory blent will go
The minstrel's lays, the minstrel's praise
   Of Anderson an' Co.

*The Purveyor
maketh answer
to the Poet. He
encloseth his bill
—twenty-first
application.*

We 've got your screed o' rhymes, lad,
　But haith ! they 're no' the thing ;
Nae sweetest note frae Poet's throat
　Outpeers the siller's ring.
Frae a' that eat our stores, lad,
　We ask a *quid pro quo* ;
The price you bid 's nae tempting quid
　To Anderson an' Co.

Your name may gang alane, lad,
　To fame o' unborn days ;
Let ours stand weel wi' ilka chiel
　That lives and eats—and pays ;
And a' that canna pay, lad,
　Our wares had best forego
They 'll draw nae ruth for purseless mooth
　Frae Anderson an' Co.

88

So never mair essay, lad,
　Wi' wild poetic throes
In crambo clink our name to link—
　We advertise in prose;
Ye've made an offer plain, lad,
　As plain 's the answer—No!
Rhymes winna please like white rupees
　John Anderson an' Co.

The Poet teareth his hair and the bill.

Curtain.

[An Indian civilian in the North-Western Provinces begins his official career by being an Assistant Magistrate and Collector, or Stunt. After that he is a Joint (that is to say, Joint Magistrate), or Junt, and then a District Magistrate and Collector, or Burra Sahib, that is to say, Great Sahib. Stunt, Junt, and Burra Sahib are terms used by natives, and they have been adopted to a great extent, like many other native renderings of English words and phrases, by Englishmen in India. 'Stunt' or 'Istunt' is the nearest approach an illiterate native can make (and they are nearly all illiterate) to the proper pronunciation of the word Assistant. 'Griff' is a Griffin, or newly-arrived youngster, fresh and green. These verses were written at a time when the prospects of 'Joints' in the North-Western Provinces were terribly black.]

Air—'*Ho! little page with dimpled chin.*'

Ho! little Stunt, with down-fledged chin,
Happy and hopeful, ruddy of cheer,

All your wish is Glory to win,
This is the way that Griffs begin,
   Wait till you come to Forty Year.

Panting to rise by prowess of brains,
   Hearing of wrong with no callous ear,
List'ning with faith and patient pains
When lying Gungadeen complains,—
   Wait till you come to Forty Year.

Twenty years o'er a Stunt's head pass,
   Fiery suns his young heart sear—
Sigheth he then, toil-spent : 'Alas !
Zeal befitted a green young ass,
   Rest is better for Forty Year.'

Pledge me round, I bid ye declare,
   'Joints' thrice ten, all grim and grey,

'JOINT' AT TWO SCORE

What of your castles built in air?
What of ambitions once your care?
   Have they not vanished all away?

Wisest they who to strive desist;
   Comes not the guerdon to worth alone:
Fluke works freaks in the Service List,
And the meed that labour and merit have
     missed,
   Falls to a fortunate dunce or drone.

Dull drag the days in a station drear,
   Dead are the dreams that pleased lang
     syne,
Dead and buried, and I sit here
A moody rhymer at Forty Year,
   Schooling a Stunt with cynic line.

THE WIDOW OF GRASS

A BACHELOR'S SONG

Air —' Here's to the Maiden of Bashful Fifteen.'

HERE's to no maiden of bashful fifteen,
   Here's to no widow of fifty :
Widows are wily, though winsome of mien,
   And maidens are skittish and shifty.
     Let the toast pass, drink to the lass,
      Nor maiden or widow, the Widow of Grass.

Old wiseacres say that the making of hay
   Should be sped in the time of the sun, sir ;

So in Ind, where, I trow, there is sunshine enow,
 The best of all things to be done, sir,
  If you'd see a day pass without yawn or 'Alas!'
  Is to go and make hay with a Widow of
   Grass.

When the hours lagging go in a station that's
   slow,
 And it's hard the blue devils to bury,
Be your mate not a wife with a face full of woe,
 But a Widow of Grass who is merry.
  Let the toast pass, filled be each glass,
  We'll drink to the health of the Widow of
   Grass.

And here's to the husband who checks not her
   whim,
 Nor tightens the conjugal tether;

94

THE WIDOW OF GRASS

Her smiles are for us, and her tempers for him,
So, faith! we'll e'en toast them together.
Let the toast pass, the husband's an ass,
A bumper for him and the Widow of Grass!

THE CIVILIAN OBADIAHS

Air—'*The Two Obadiahs.*'

SAID the young Obadiah to the old Obadiah :
   'You're a judge, Obadiah, you're a judge,
And judges old as you are for pension overdue,
   You should budge, Obadiah, you should budge
The measure of your years is full, your labours
     now should cease,
So hie you to an English home, there end your
     days in peace,
And take the blessings with you of the friends
     you'll leave behind.'
       Said the old Obadiah,
        'You are kind.'

96

Said the young Obadiah to the old Obadiah,
  ‘ You are stout, apoplectically stout ;
And before the rains last year you were very,
    very near
  Going out, Obadiah, going out.
With that warning to remember, with a phiz of
    tell-tale hue,
After many a shock of fever and of liver not a few,
Yet, yet another summer will you dare your fate
    defy ? ’
        Growled the old Obadiah,
          ‘ I will try.’

Said the young Obadiah to the old Obadiah,
  ‘ I ’m a Joint, Obadiah, still a Joint,
And ’twill dam Promotion’s flow if you Seniors
    ripe to go
  Disappoint, Obadiah, disappoint.

From happier times your service dates, before the
    blank to-day
Of elderly Assistants and Joints whose heads are
    grey.
So I'm thinking, Obadiah, you have laid some
    money by.'
        Swore the old Obadiah,
          'Not a pie.' [1]

Said the young Obadiah to the old Obadiah,
    'I've a son, Obadiah, I've a son.'
Said the old Obadiah to the young Obadiah,
    'D'ye think, Obadiah, I have none?
I have three; they're gay young loafers, who
    dance and shoot and ride,

---

[1] Twelve pies go to the anna, and sixteen annas to the rupee.
This last coin, which was once worth two shillings or more,
is now equivalent to a shilling or so.

THE CIVILIAN OBADIAHS

And beyond such pleasant pastimes take thought
    of nought beside,
All three without a calling, and what's more,
    with none in view.'
       Said the young Obadiah,
         ' Rough on you.'

Said the young Obadiah to the old Obadiah,
   ' I 've a wife, Obadiah, I 've a wife.'
Said the old Obadiah to the young Obadiah,
   ' So have I, Obadiah, bless your life !
'Twould move your ruth, my gentle youth, if
    you only saw the bills
Of my Mrs. Obadiah and her daughters in the
    hills.
Five daughters, Obadiah, and no husbands to be
    had.'
       Said the young Obadiah,
         ' That is sad.'

Said the old Obadiah to the young Obadiah,
  ''Twould be well, Obadiah, don't you think,
Lest our throttles get too dry with question and
    reply,
  If we moistened the discussion with a drink!'
With zest young Obadiah caught the Senior's
    notion up,
Fetched a giant tankard straightway, filled it
    high with Simkin[1] cup,
Added herbs of fine aroma, crowned the whole
    with crystal ice,—
      Smiled the old Obadiah,
        ''Twill be nice.'

Then the old Obadiah and the young Obadiah
  Sat them down, chair by chair, *tête-à-tête* ;
But, curious to say, all remembrance passed away
  Of the interesting topic of debate.

      [1] 'Simkin'=Champagne.

Soon the young Obadiah, with his glass raised
    high,
Was carolling the ditties of his infancy :
While the old Obadiah wore a look of wild
    delight,
        And chortled, ' Obadiah,
            You are tight.'

Still sat the heroes two, still happier they
    grew,
    As they drained the giant tankard o'er and
    o'er :
Till at last—O sad to tell !—old Obadiah fell
    In a leaden, leaden slumber on the floor.
Then crowed the wily Junior, ' Not in vain I
    primed it strong ;
My venerable friend, I think, won't stop pro-
    motion long,

At least not if as often as he wants to liquor
up
He lets young Obadiah
Mix the cup!'

YE BANKS AND BRAES O' DEHRA DOON

Air—' Ye banks and braes o' bonnie Doon.'

[Mussoorie, a favourite hill station, is in the district of
Dehra Doon.]

YE banks and braes o' Dehra Doon,
  Bloom, bloom no more sae fresh and fair :
Mussoorie youths, companions boon,
  Carouse not now when I forbear.

Thou Mall where Amazons display
  Their fearless grace on palfries restive,
Desist, in Love's own name, I pray,
  From looking so intensely festive.

103

Ye haunts, ye walks that once I knew,
   When life and I alike were jolly,—
I'm altered now : oblige me, do,
   By looking meetly melancholy.

'Twas love that erst my joy did cause,
   'Tis love that now my joy has ta'en,
And ever doth the joy that was
   Embitter more the after pain.

Fond, fond the rapture of my soul
   That night when from the ballroom's glare
With sweet Selina forth I stole,
   To breathe the witching midnight air.

The scene, the time, to love beguiled,
   The night was still, the moon was up,
The stars rained down their influence mild,—
   And I'd been drinking Simkin cup.

O' DEHRA DOON

My bosom, deeply stirred with love,
  In fear now shook, with hope now swelled,
To still the fear, the hope to prove,
  I craved a thorny rose she held.

She answered with assenting look ;
  Her yielding hand in mine I drew,
And as the token flower I took
  I deemed the hand my guerdon too.

Oh, faithless as the shifting sand !
  Short weeks have sped but barely three ;
She's given old General Gudge her hand,
  The rose—and thorns—are left to me !

LAMENT OF THE SETTLEMENT OFFICERS

' Quhen Alysander our kyng was dede.'

An extract, with some slight modifications, from an article in *The University Magazine,* now extinct, will serve as a preface to these verses.

The Settlement Officers (see the ' Hakim Bundobust ') make the periodical assessments of the Government Land Revenue in India. In the North-Western Provinces a re-valuation ordinarily takes place every thirty years. There was a great deal of work of this kind to be done when Sir William Muir was Lieutenant-Governor of the North-West, and civilians, specially selected, were employed on it. Sir William Muir spoke of them in a debate in the Legislative Council as ' the picked men of a picked service.' The civilians who were not selected did not like this, and a jester—of course, one of the Settlement Staff

—ticketed them as 'the piqued men of a piqued service.' The work of settlement is partly outdoor, in the way of survey and inspection, and partly desk work, consisting of drawing up reports. The outdoor work is naturally limited in duration to the cold weather, or the months from November to February inclusive. Sir William Muir, in his indulgence for his 'picked men,' thought that they might as well do their desk work in a cool climate, and gave them permission to migrate to Naini Tal in the hills in the hot weather. Arrived there, they had a choice of recreations in which they could indulge, in addition to, or instead of, writing Assessment Reports. When Sir William Muir retired and Sir John Strachey reigned in his stead, a rumour went forth (which turned out to be substantially true) that the Settlement Staff were no longer to have the same liberty as before of taking flight to the hills in the hot weather.

Jwalakhet and Cheena are the names of places at or near Naini Tal.

Wo! Willie Muir, our kynge, is deid!
We ken nae mair his favourin' ee;

LAMENT OF SETTLEMENT OFFICERS

Gane are our days of generous meed,
   Of wine and wassail, games and glee;
O gentle hevin! grant remede,
   And shield us frae the cauld Straychee.

Our Willie dear in switherin mood
   Full aft wi' doubt wad wrestle sair,
Yet still to us a patron good
   Proclaimed our ends his ceaseless care;
Had we been e'en his kin in blood
   He couldna weel hae loved us mair.

Whate'er we penned, in many a screed,
   Much cry about a little woo',
He printed for the warld to read
   In beuks o' yellow, beuks o' blue,
And crowning proof of love indeed,
   Himself he read them, through and through.

LAMENT OF SETTLEMENT OFFICERS

And if our eggs of settlement
  [As chanced at times through Fortune's spite]
For all the years in hatching spent,
  Proved addled when they saw the light,
He smiled on them with mild content
  As sweet and sound and flawless quite.

From out the herd he did us raise,
  And, guiding still our favoured feet,
Far sundered from the rest our ways,
  And gave, by a division meet,
To us the guerdon and the praise,
  To them the burden and the heat:

And therefore when, from dust and glare,
  His court did its departure take,
And glad to summer haunt repair
  On Nynee's hills, by Nynee's lake

LAMENT OF SETTLEMENT OFFICERS

Us too he bid attend him there
　　For our transcendant merits' sake.

Soon, heedless of Assessment notes,
　　Wi' lichtsome hearts we flung them doun,
And sallied forth in soldiers' coats
　　To march wi' martial show and soun',
And rowed the lake in bonnie boats,
　　And leapt and sprang at Badmintoune.

With bullets' ring in Jwalakhet
　　Our rifles roused the echoes clear,
On piny steeps, in gorges strait,
　　We sought at dawn the mountain deer,
In Cheena's dells at eve we sat,
　　And whispered love in beauty's ear.

O sad, O dismal change ! at last
　　The common lot of ills we share,

LAMENT OF SETTLEMENT OFFICERS

Erst deemed but nightmares of the past,
   And all the harder now to bear,—
The breath of June's sirocco blast,
   The weight of August's leaden air.

And that the altered doom we dree
   May lack no sting of jest and jeer,
The Great Unpicked, with ribald glee,
   Triumphantly their crests uprear,
And loud extol the cauld Straychee,
   And cavil at our Willie dear.

But let them mock with rancour vain,
   We, sad of heart and fain to greet,
Will none the less in pious strain
   The chorus of his praise repeat :
Where shall we see his like again,
   Our Willie lost, our Willie sweet?

ALUN AHEER

Air—'*Allen-a-Dale*'—Scott's *Rokeby*.

ALUN AHEER has no tillage for tending,
Alun Aheer has no hoards for the lending,
Alun Aheer has no wares for the selling,
Yet Alun Aheer has rich stores beyond telling.
Ye law-loving gentlemen, please you to hear
What manner of craftsman is Alun Aheer!

He vaunteth no manors, no heirlooms of pride;
No henchman, to serve him, attends at his side;
He has naught but his lathie,[1] good five cubits
    long;
His foot that is fleet, and his hand that is strong;

[1] Lathie—A long bamboo cudgel.

ALUN AHEER

A head passing wily, a heart without fear,
Yet he laugheth at fortune, blithe Alun Aheer.

There are tools he must use in his time-honoured
    trade,
That gold never purchased and hand never made ;
His cudgel, it 's true, for a song you may buy,
But the heart, skill, and sinew his cudgel to ply,
To fight like the panther, to scud like the deer,
Are sold in no market, saith Alun Aheer.

Dear, dear to the miser the coffers that hold
His treasure of silver, his jewels and gold ;
He calls them his own, but in truth and in deed
He keeps them for Alun, to take at his need ;
Some morrow he 'll wail o'er his night-ravished
    gear,
Gone—none can say whither, but Alun Aheer.

They're proud of their acres, your husbandry
men,
The lord has his thousand, the hind has his ten;
But the broad earth is Alun's, the East and the
West,
The Northward, the Southward, to choose of the
best;
Though the harvest be scanty, the rents in
arrear,
There still must be tithage for Alun Aheer.

Through the green meadow lowlands as Alun
doth hie,
It's woe to the herdsman that's drowsy of eye;
Ah! well may he spring from his sleep with a
start,
And number the kine with a sinking of heart,

114

For gone is their leader, the best-beloved steer,
Far, far o'er the Ganges with Alun Aheer.

But the game that's the crown of bold Alun's
    desire
Is cracking of costards for pastime or hire ;
When a fat Kayath landlord would serve out a
    foe,
The greasy old craven to Alun doth go,
Gives a hint of a name with a wink and a leer,
Then away with his lathic goes Alun Aheer.

Anon he returneth, his mission is sped,
And his cudgel of vengeance is dinted and red ;
Then, faith, if there's slackness in finding the
    price,
He 'll drub the old Kayath himself in a trice,

And teach him—the niggard!—it costs rather
    dear
To bilk of his wages bold Alun Aheer.

Is he taken red-hand at his head-breaking sport?
He has clansmen a score who'll attend him in
    court,
And swear he lay sleeping, the hour of the fray,
At his wife's cousin's grandmother's—ten leagues
    away.
They mock at your oaths, so outlandish and
    queer,
And lie without wincing for Alun Aheer.

Is he scourged with the rod?—fixed as iron his
    face,
Though each blow writes a gash, and he bleedeth
    apace ;

ALUN AHEER

The paly-skinned Brahmin will clamour and
    bawl
Ere the cords can be tied, or the rattan can
    fall;
But you'll lay on till doom ere to pleading or
    tear
Be bent the bold spirit of Alun Aheer.

Is the halter his fate?—yet his cheek grows not
    pale,
His step will not falter, his eye will not quail;
One word to his dark-eyed Aheerin he saith,
Then mounts like a king up the ladder to
    death,—
Ever dauntless of heart, ever lightsome of
    cheer,
As his life will his death be, our Alun Aheer!

There's a plea for his acts, though you brand
 them as crimes,
In the mouth he was born with, that hungers at
 times;
And Alun doth argue with reason unskilled,
That when God gives a mouth it is meant to be
 filled;
So he fills it, in sooth, with what's handy and
 near—
' Lest God be offended,' saith Alun Aheer.

If Alun's a reaver, Sirkar[1] is the same,
Though not by one method they tend to their
 aim;
Sirkar works by law, in a sinuous way,
And scribbles and prates ere it springs on its
 prey,

   [1] 'Sirkar'=the Government.

118

ALUN AHEER

While our thief to his end driveth sudden and
    sheer;
Is Sirkar then more honest than Alun Aheer?

As to which is loved best—let the Thakur reply,
Whom your law and the bunneah have bled till
     he's dry;
Ask the multitude, weary to death of the rule
That cleanses and counts them and hounds them
     to school;
Ask the trader taxed bare of the gains of a year
If Sirkar is more gentle than Alun Aheer?

With your statutes and laws you have cumbered
     the land,
Till there's barely a spot for poor Alun to stand,
And you foster not him, but the sycophant breed
Who drive for a pittance in ink-dabbled reed;

What duty, then, owes he your laws to revere?
Let those keep them who made them, not Alun
    Aheer.

You can kill him, you think, but he'll leave you
    a son
Whose pride is to do as his father has done;
And again when your harvests are stripped in
    the night,
And the dawn finds the usurer's money-bags
    light,
And gardens are plundered, and kine disappear,
You'll swear he's new-risen, dead Alun Aheer.

My singing is o'er—they have heard not in vain
Who will join as in chorus this close to the
    strain :—

Be there death to the loon who with sycophant's
    heart
Will cringe to the Hakim[1] he hates in his heart,
But live the frank outlaw, our thief without peer,
The pink of all robbers, bold Alun Aheer!

[1] 'Hakim'= Ruler, Magistrate.

DIDO ANGLO-INDICA

'A weary lot is thine, fair maid.'—Scott.

'A BOOTLESS game is thine, sweet lass,
    A bootless game is thine!
To snatch at hearts of men that pass
    The way you snatched at mine!
As many others come, I came
    This Eastern land to view;
You learnt I bore a titled name,
    No more of me you knew,
        My love!
    No more of me you knew.

122

' Three fateful moons have seen us run
    Through love's delights and pains;
So much we've said, so much we've done,
    To part alone remains.'
He gave her hand a farewell shake,
    To kiss, unkind, forbore;
' The next home mail I fain must take,
    So adieu for evermore,
        My love!
    Adieu for evermore.'

C.S.I. AND C.I.E.

Air—'*County Guy.*'

[In the eyes of aspirants for Indian decorations the Knighthoods and Companionships of the Star of India have much higher value than the corresponding grades of the Order of the Indian Empire. A C.I.E.-ship, in particular, is looked upon as 'the wooden spoon' among titular honours. One worthy old gentleman, on being made a *homo trium litterarum* of the C.I.E. sort, was comforted by a sympathising friend in the words, 'Never mind, old fellow, you'll live it down.' In 1890 two deserving Civil Servants, whose names were (something like) Bede and Blees, were branded C.I.E. at the same time as a number of natives of sorts.]

An, C.S.I., I thought thee nigh,
And said : ' This year's *Gazette*
'Mid other names my signal claims
Will surely not forget.'

124

C.S.I. AND C.I.E.

The list appeared : I hoped, yet feared,
    And read with fevered haste ;
O fate too hard ! Amongst the starred
    I found my name—not placed.

Then lower down with listless eye
    I read the C.I.E.'s,
A Singh, a Khan, a Rao, a Rai,
    And Messrs. Bede and Blees.
' Poor Bede! poor Blees!' consoled, I cry,
    ' Worse off than I are ye,
Far better miss a C.S.I.
    Than win a C.I.E.!'

BRUCE'S ADDRESS—NEW VERSION

Air—'*Scots wha hae.*'

[This address was supposed to be delivered by a Bruce,
the Earl of Elgin, Viceroy of India, to the Scots-
men assembled at a St. Andrew's dinner in
Calcutta.]

Scots on halesome parritch bred,

Scots in black coats, Scots in red,

Scots whose sires for mine hae bled,

Fill the cup wi' me !

Holy Andrew's sainted pow'r

Rules the day an' rules the hour,

Smooths each brow wi' care knit sour,

Stirs to jollitie.

126

BRUCE'S ADDRESS—NEW VERSION

Wha frae drinkin' like the lave,
Feckless, wad exemption crave,
Clootie grup the loon an' knave!
    Here he maunna be!

Wha amang us, great or sma',
Fair drinks doon his brethren a',
First to fill and last to fa',
    Haith! our king is he!

Scotia's drink, the pibroch's strains,
Thrill our heart-strings, fire our veins;
Scottish faithers' Scottish weans,
    Wha sae prood as we!

Loud the Norlan' trumpet blow!
Wha like us to do or know!
Dings the best the warl' can show,
    Scotland's chivalrie!

COURTS of Justice in India are insulted every day, almost every hour, by the most shameless perjuries. A false *alibi* is one of the most recurring forms of this pest. Half a dozen witnesses are produced as a matter of course, to swear that a man who has been clearly shown by the evidence for the prosecution to have committed a murder at Pacchamabad was at Purabpur when the deed was done. Their evidence is solemnly recorded by the Sessions Judge. The proceedings remind one of nothing so much as the vulgar verse—

> ' I saw Esau kissing Kate,
> And the fact is we all three saw,
> For I saw Esau, he saw me,
> And she saw I saw Esau.'

The Judge knows the evidence he is writing down is false. The learned Government pleader and the

128

able counsel for the defence know it is false, and they both know the Judge knows it is false. But the farce of listening to it, and recording it, and cross-examining and re-examining on it, must be gone through, in deference to the requirements of the *Code of Criminal Procedure.*

Fortunately, the fabrication of *alibis* is a disease which has to some extent cured itself. Over-production has had the usual result of bringing about a depreciation in value. *Alibis* are so common that Courts hold them very cheap. But a monstrous amount of time is wasted in examining the lying witnesses who come forward to support them. And an *alibi* constructed with more than usual care sometimes turns the scale against the prosecution, and saves a rascal from the punishment he deserves. The cross-examination of witnesses who are called to prove a well-constructed *alibi* is of very little use. Say that a murder is committed on the 7th of May. On the morning of the 8th the murderer starts off on a pilgrimage to Brindaban with half a dozen of his friends and kinsmen. The half-dozen are called as witnesses for the defence at the trial, and swear that they and the accused started for Brindaban on 6th of May, and were there the whole of the 7th. It is useless to cross-examine them with regard to the incidents of the pilgrimage, for it is a real fact, and they will agree as regards every detail. The alteration of the date of starting is the only lie, and that lie is unanimously stuck to. The lying witnesses stand to their guns unshaken, and leave the Court with beaming faces, well pleased with the figure they have cut; and the chances are a hundred to one—so over-burdened are Courts in India with work—against their ever being punished, or even tried, for perjury.

APPENDIX II

JUSTICE *à LA* BRIDOYE FOR INDIA

THERE was once upon a time a very worthy Judge who was called before the High Court of his Province to explain his reasons for having pronounced an apparently inequitable sentence in a case before him. His explanation was that, during a long and honourable career on the Bench, his practice had been to determine cases by throwing dice after reading the pleadings, hearing counsel, and carefully weighing the evidence. Having first carried out all the formalities of procedure, he used to lay on his table all the papers filed by the defendant, and give him the first chance with the dice. That done, he laid down at the other end of the table the papers filed by the plaintiff or complainant, and gave him his chance. In simple cases large dice were used, but in those which, from the number of papers filed, appeared to be difficult and intricate, the casts were made with specially small and delicate dice. The Judge excused himself with regard to the particular case under inquiry on the ground that his sight, not being so good as it had been, he could not distinctly discern the points of the dice as formerly, so that it might have happened that, at the decision of the cause in question, in which he had used his small dice, he had mistaken a quatre for a cinque, and thereby given an erroneous judgment. The presiding Chief-Justice asked Judge Bridoye [for that was his name] why, as he gave his judgment according to the cast of the dice, he did not throw the hazards at once, without troubling himself with documents or with the arguments of counsel. It would take up too much space to give Judge Bridoye's ingenious and conclusive answers to this and other questions. Those who are desirous of knowing what they were, and of learning the issue of the proceedings, will find a full account of them in the delectable *History of Pantagruel,* by François Rabelais.[1]

My own object is to call attention to the eminent adaptability of the Bridoye method to the conditions of judicial work in India, in which, as is well known to all persons who have had any experience of Courts, the decision of cases by a laborious consideration of evidence is an empty and delusive mockery. And

[1] See 'The Case of Judge Bridoye' in Sir Walter Besant's *Readings in Rabelais.*

132

I would remind my readers that the principle
of the Bridoye method has not been unfamiliar in
the past, although there have been differences in
the mode of putting it in practice. Every one has
heard of the Judge who used to decide his cases by
counting the flies on the punkah-frame, and decreeing
for the plaintiff if the number was odd, and for the
defendant if it was even. This plan has its recommen-
dations, but it is open to the objection that there are
seasons in the year when punkah-frames are taken
down, and during which there would be a difficulty in
securing the attendance of a sufficient number of flies.
Then there was the judicial officer who was deputed
to a district in which there was an immense mass of
appeals of old-standing to be disposed of. He
ordered the records to be laid out in cutcherry, and,
making use of his walking-stick as a divining-rod,
touched first one file and then another, giving orders
for decrees for plaintiff and defendant alternately.
The Serishtadar[1] wrote out good reasons, supported
by apposite rulings of the Allahabad High Court, for
each decree. The Judge signed them, and the arrears
melted away in a marvellously short space of time. I
cite these instances merely to show I am not recom-

---

[1] 'Serishtadar '=Head Clerk.

mending any absolutely unheard-of innovation of principle.

The advantages that would flow from the adoption of the Bridoye method would be many and various. Judicial work would be more speedily despatched. No longer worried by laborious balancing of perjured evidence, civil officers would less frequently become deranged in intellect than now. Their tempers would be sweeter. They would have more leisure to show kindness to the natives of the country. In the veracity and standard of honesty of the latter there would soon be a marked improvement; perjury and forgery, being of use no longer for the bewilderment of Judges, would cease to be habitually practised.

Hasty reasoners will be likely to argue that justice would not be attained under the Bridoye system. It is not difficult to show that in courts of every grade the results would be as satisfactory as under the existing system; nay, more so. Take, for instance, the Allahabad High Court, the rulings of which are held in deservedly high estimation, not only in these provinces, but throughout the length and breadth of India. There have been twenty reported cases of appeals from its decisions to the Privy Council since the Indian Law Reports were first published. In ten of these the decisions appealed against have been confirmed. In an equal number they have been reversed.[1] It would appear, therefore, that the justice dispensed by our respected High Court is so strictly even-handed that in any given case before it there are equal chances that the decision will be wise, equal chances that it will be otherwise. And, these being the chances in the High Court, it may be assumed that in the courts of subordinate, and of course less able, judges, there is at least a shade of odds against a right decision being given. Now in every case tried according to the Bridoye method, the party who ought to win would have as good a chance as the party who ought to lose: that is to say, the chances of justice being done would invariably be even. In the High Court, therefore, the results would be no less satisfactory, and in subordinate courts they would be more so than those attained under the existing system. This being so, and there being collateral advantages besides, is there not a strong case for the adoption of the Bridoye method in courts in India, and may we not hope that His Excellency the Viceroy, who is always so ready to promote wise reforms, will take note of and consider these suggestions?

[1] These were the results up to the time when the above remarks were written.

APPENDIX III

APPEAL OF THE ELDERS IN THE STRANGE CASE
OF SUSANNA: AN ANCIENT LAW REPORT

[This law report appeared in the *Pioneer* towards the close
of a period of unrest and perplexity for judicial officers in the
North-West Provinces, when the Judges of the Allahabad
High Court were interfering far too freely, and often on very
captious grounds, with the proceedings of Magistrates and
Sessions Judges. The advent of Sir John Edge wrought a
most salutary change in this respect. From the time of his
assumption of the office of Chief-Justice an era began in
which substantial justice has been done, and the dictates
of common-sense have prevailed rather than ultra-legal
quirks and quibbles.]

THE great advance which has been made of late
years in the interpretation of cuneiform writing is
well-known to Oriental scholars. The successful
labours of Professor Zurmach, of the Leipsic University, in that interesting field of research, enable us
to lay before our readers the following extract from
the weekly notes of cases decided by the High Court,
Babylon, in the Chaldæan year 86 :—

136

APPEAL OF THE ELDERS

Before the Officiating Chief-Justice and Mr. Justice Bahpoohd.

CRIMINAL APPEAL, No. 9999.

THE KING *v.* BADOLDLOT AND BADEROLDLOT.

The Officiating Chief-Justice.—This is an appeal against a decision of the Sessions Judge of Babylon convicting the appellants, Badoldlot and Baderoldlot, under section 211 of the Medo-Persian Penal Code, of making a false charge against Susanna, wife of Joacim. The case arises out of a previous case tried by the bench of magistrates exercising jurisdiction in the Jewish quarter in Babylon. In that case Susanna was accused of abetting the commission of an offence under section 411 of the Medo-Persian Penal Code, by dishonestly handing over certain jewels, the property of her husband, to a person unknown, who received them with a guilty knowledge. Proceedings were taken against Susanna on information furnished by the present appellants. She was acquitted, and sanction was given to the prosecution of the appellants for making a false charge. The Sessions Judge convicted them, and sentenced them to the severest punishment that could be inflicted under the law.

The first observation I have to make is that the procedure of the learned Sessions Judge, in trying the two appellants together instead of separately, was contrary to the purport of repeated rulings of this court. Each of the two accused should have been separately tried, so as to give him the benefit of the evidence of the other as a witness. The irregularity of trying them together would alone be a sufficient reason for quashing the sentences passed. It is further to be remarked that there was no evidence whatever against the appellants beyond the fact that they fell into a contradiction, or what was assumed to be a contradiction, when cross-examined by the counsel for the defence in the case against Susanna. Badoldlot stated that he saw Susanna handing over her husband's jewels to the receiver in her husband's garden *under a holm tree,* and Baderoldlot said he saw her do so *under a mastick tree.* I am unable to adopt the view that there was any necessary contradiction between the two statements. There is no evidence in the record to show that Badoldlot and Baderoldlot were speaking with reference to precisely the same point of time. It is not impossible that Susanna may have handed over some of her husband's jewels under a holm tree and others under a mastick tree. She may have met the receiver in the first instance under a holm tree, and then, before the handing over of the jewels was completed, have withdrawn with him to a more secluded spot under a mastick tree, in which case both of the appellants may have been speaking the truth. And even if their statements related to the same point of time, it is possible that there is a spot in the garden where a holm tree and a mastick tree grow close together. Susanna and the receiver may have been standing beneath the interlacing boughs of the two trees, and Badoldlot may have said with perfect good faith that the jewels were handed over under a holm tree, and Baderoldlot, with equal good faith, that they were handed over under a mastick tree. And even if there is no place in the garden where a holm tree and a mastick tree stand close together, and the appellants were speaking, or meant to speak, about the same tree, one or both of them may have been under a mistake as to the kind of tree. The Government prosecutor, who appears in support of the conviction, admits with great candour that he does not know the distinguishing features of a holm tree or a mastick tree, and I feel bound to say that I myself am equally ignorant on the subject. Badoldlot and Baderoldlot, as appears from the Sessions Record, are natives of the most central quarter of Babylon—that in which the temples of the dragon Bo and the god Bel are situated. The inhabitants of this quarter, who reside in the immediate neighbourhood of the two temples, and within hearing of the cornet, flute, harp, psaltery, and dulcimer, and all kinds of music by which the votaries of Bo and Bel are summoned to worship, are regarded as peculiarly the citizens of Babylon : so much so that it has passed into a proverb that those only are true Babylonians who are ' born within the sound of Bo Bel.' It is notorious that Babylonians who fall under this category know little or nothing of the appearance of the common objects of the country, amongst which I consider that trees may fairly be held to be included. It is possible, therefore, that Badoldlot and Baderoldlot, having been ' born within the sound of Bo Bel,' may be as incapable of recognising a holm tree or a mastick tree when they see one as myself or the able Government prosecutor, and the contradiction on which so much stress has been laid may have been the result of a mistake. The probability that there was a mistake is enhanced by the consideration that if Susanna went to the garden to wash herself [and this was her story] she no doubt selected a spot which was sheltered by a tree : and it would have been easy for the appellants, if they had been conspiring to make a false charge, and were able to tell one tree from another, to arrange to name the tree she washed herself under as the tree under which she handed over the jewels.

Even if it be assumed that there is no basis of fact for any one of the hypotheses which I have suggested: that is to say, if the statements of Badoldlot and Baderoldlot related to the same point of time; if there are no two trees standing close together, of one of which Badoldlot could have been speaking while Baderoldlot spoke of the other; and if both of them are quite capable of telling a holm tree or a mastick tree when they see one, still the fact of the contradiction, though it may prove that one of them must have made a false statement, does not necessarily prove that they both did. Badoldlot may have stated truly what he really saw, and Baderoldlot may have made a false statement, or *vice versa*. It is possible that one only of them made a false statement. Evidence which goes no further than the fact of contradiction [assuming that there was really and truly a contradiction not resulting from a mistake] does not prove which of the two appellants made a false statement, if one of them did, and it was obviously improper to convict both of them on evidence which was conclusive against neither.

If Susanna had been examined as a witness, and had denied on oath that she gave any jewels to any person in the garden, and her evidence had been believed, there would then have been a legal basis for a finding that Badoldlot and Baderoldlot were both guilty of making a false charge. But Susanna was not examined at all. The Sessions Judge accepted as true, apparently as a matter of course, the interested statements made by her as an accused person in the previous trial, which was, of course, highly improper. Besides, even if Susanna had been examined as a witness, I am not prepared to say that it would have been safe to convict the appellants, or either of them, on her uncorroborated evidence. It appears from the record of the case against her that the statements of the appellants were borne out to this extent, that it was admitted that Susanna came to the garden, and that she then sent away two female servants who had accompanied her there. Those two servants were not called as witnesses to support her statement that she had come to the garden with the innocent and praiseworthy intention of washing herself. If it was true, as she stated, that she sent them away to bring oil and

washing-balls, why were they not called as witnesses to
say so? There is evidence that they returned to the
garden after the appellants had seen Susanna there;
but it does not appear that they came with oil and
washing-balls. Susanna, who has been present at
the hearing of this appeal, and is a lady of consider-
able personal attractions, is not now on trial, and I
have no wish to cast the slightest imputation on her
veracity; but I feel it my duty, in fairness to the
appellants, to take notice of what may be called the
significant omission on the part of her legal adviser to
call her two female servants as witnesses for her in the
previous case.

The appellants adduced evidence to show that they
have hitherto borne a high character, and have held an
influential position in the Jewish community. They
are county councillors for the Jewish ward of the city
of Babylon, and have evinced an active interest in the
development of local self-government; they are men
of means, and have assisted with liberal subscriptions
the movement lately set on foot by the leaders of the
Medo-Persian community for supplying every Jewish
mother of a family with a tooth-brush and a pocket-
handkerchief, articles which, owing to sentiments of
modesty deserving the highest respect, Jewish ladies

have hitherto refrained from using. The previous
good character and high respectability of the appellants
must count for something in weighing the probabilities
of the case.

I observe with much regret that, in the trial of the
original case against Susanna, the bench of magistrates
allowed a most extraordinary and reprehensible licence
to the counsel for the accused. The record shows that
he was permitted to address the appellant Badoldlot,
who was then a witness for the prosecution, in the
words, 'Thou seed of Canaan and not of Judah.'
In the first place, it does not appear that the fact of
his being 'seed of Canaan and not of Judah,' if proved,
would necessarily have affected his credibility. In
the next place, the cross-examining counsel ought not
to have been allowed to address the witness as if the
fact suggested had been established by evidence. The
way in which the appellant Baderoldlot was permitted
to be addressed was even more improper—indeed, it
was nothing short of outrageous. Susanna's counsel
began his cross-examination of Baderoldlot by address-
ing him in these words: 'O thou that art waxed old
in wickedness.' An imputation couched in such
opprobrious terms must necessarily have discom-
posed a witness who, up to that time, had borne an

unblemished reputation, and may have had a serious effect in incapacitating him from calmly recollecting under what kind of tree the matters to which he deposed had taken place.

The conclusion I come to, after most careful consideration, is that the whole case teems with possibilities throwing doubt on the guilt of the appellants. Of that doubt, in accordance with the unalterable usage of Medo-Persian law, particularly when administered by a High Court, they should be allowed the benefit. The order, therefore, which I propose to pass is that the convictions be quashed, and that the appellants be set at liberty.

Bahpoohd, J.—I fully concur in the conclusions of the learned Chief-Justice and in the order he proposes to pass; but as there is a difference in the steps of ratiocination by which I have arrived at the same results, I feel obliged *ex necessitate* to say something in explanation of my *ratio decidendi* in the case. For this purpose it will, first of all, be necessary for me to consider the words *false* and *charge* in their legal and colloquial sense. I shall then proceed to set forth my views at some length, in accordance with the judicial maxims, *parvum in multo* and *ex monte mus*, on all the recorded cases of making a false charge since the creation of the world. I regret that I have been unable to find any reported case of date anterior to the Deluge. Subsequent thereto there is the well-known case, Joseph *v.* Zuleikha, wife of Potiphar. The ruling in that . . .

[The law report was here brought to a sudden close by the following editorial note. It should be mentioned that the judgments of Mr. Mahmood, one of the Puisne Judges of the Allahabad High Court, were as much distinguished for being voluminous as luminous :—]

'We regret that the space available in our issue of to-day does not admit of our printing the remainder of Mr. Justice Bahpoohd's luminous judgment, which extends to about ten times the dimensions of that of the Babylonian officiating Chief-Justice. We hope, perhaps, to be able to find room for it on some future date, should we ever happen to have no home politics, no Eastern question, no brushes with Dacoits in Burma, no discussions regarding the depreciation of the rupee, no Service grievances—in fact, no matter of any ordinary kind to fill our columns.—*Ed.*'

Printed by T. and A. CONSTABLE, Printers to Her Majesty
at the Edinburgh University Press

www.ingramcontent.com/pod-product-compliance
Lightning Source LLC
Chambersburg PA
CBHW021127020726
47500CB00003B/963